Tea O'clock

A wizard-plumbing-disaster
Adventure

*To my brother,
the wizard we all deserve.*

First published in 2021 by Twilight Cat

Copyright © Atticus Ryder

ISBN 978-1-8380956-4-2

Also available as an ebook

ISBN 978-1-8380956-5-9

Edited and proof read by Alice Corrie.
Typeset by Clair Lansley.

Tea O'clock

A wizard-plumbing-disaster
Adventure

Atticus Ryder

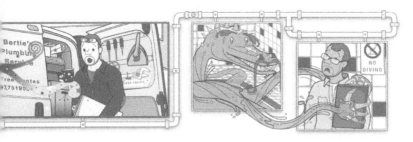

CoNtents

Chapter 1

LaTe!

Bong!

Percy snorted then slowly leant into the side of his comfy old armchair.

Bong! The grandfather clock chimed again. Louder this time.

His eyelids fluttered.

Bong!

'It was the elephant on the orange sofa,' Percy mumbled in his sleep, 'he nibbled the chocolate off the top!'

Bong-bong-bong!

'Alright, alright, I'm awake!' Percy yawned,

although his eyes were still closed.

'About time!' the Grandfather Clock grumbled. 'I've been chiming for thirteen minutes.'

'Must you talk so loudly?' Percy grumbled.

He was in his living room. Piles of books and papers littered every surface. Empty plates and tea cups were all around. Percy had been sleeping in his favourite high-backed chair, next to the fireplace. The rest of the furniture had a friendly, worn look. On the walls, hung his wizarding and witching family portraits. At first, he'd wondered why his sister, Drusilla, had insisted he should take them when he left home, but now, looking up at their disapproving faces, he understood. *At least they were good company*, he thought.

'You've only got yourself to blame,' the Grandfather Clock continued, 'you're the one that put a spell on me. Wake me up, you said.'

'Is it seven o'clock already?' asked Percy, squinting in the bright sunlight as the curtains opened by themselves.

'Actually it's thirteen minutes past nine,' said the Grandfather Clock.

'*Nine thirteen!* I thought I spelled the alarm for seven. I'm going to be late. Again!'

Percy shot up and nearly tripped over his robe.

'You did, but then you're not very good at magic!'

'I agree,' shouted a voice from the hallway.

'Oh, not you as well, Magnus,' sighed Percy, then he pulled his blue pointy hat down, walked over to the mirror in the hallway and looked at the bags under his eyes. Two swirling eyes and a wide mouth appeared on the silvery surface.

'You look particularly dreadful this morning,' said Magnus.

Percy raised an eyebrow.

'Morning to you too,' he said. 'Much as I'd like to, Magnus, I haven't got time to swap compliments. I need to get going now if I want to get to the nursing home in time for mid-morning tea.'

'But you said you'd polish me this morning,' Magnus moaned, 'I'm dusty!'

'I know, I know. I will. Later. I promise.'

'Fat chance,' grumbled Magnus Magnus and rolled his eyes. 'You said you'd redecorate last month and look at my wall! I have to hang here all day you know.'

Percy tugged at the peeling floral wallpaper, then pulled his stick-like wand out and grinned.

'I could always use a spell to do it!'

'No!' Magnus replied quickly. 'Really, it's fine. Just a good old-fashioned polish when you're ready, please.'

'Suit yourself,' smiled Percy.

'Don't forget to brush your teeth!' Magnus reminded him.

After swinging open the bathroom door, Percy stared down in panic. There was a large puddle of brown liquid on the floor. *Oh no!* he thought, *I hope that's not what I think it is!* Percy gingerly bent down and sniffed at it. *Phew, not poo!* he thought with relief, but it was something he could really do without when he was already running late. He had a quick look to see if he could work out what was up. There was nothing obvious, so he decided to call a plumber.

He tiptoed around the puddle, brushed his teeth, then fished out his wand from his top pocket and held it out.

'*Wand.* Call a plumber.'

The Wand vibrated and purple sparks fizzed out of the top.

'A plum is a soft fruit and cannot receive calls. Did you mean, call your mum?' replied the Wand.

'Yes, I know what a plum is, you silly . . . '

'Dialling your mum,' the Wand interrupted.

'No! Stop,' Percy shouted. 'Finish. *End.* I don't have time to talk to my mum!'

'How can I help you today? Would you like a plum?' the Wand replied.

Percy rolled his eyes and cleared his throat.

'Please *call* a Plumb-*ER*.'

The Wand paused, then fizzed again.

'Dialling a local plumber.'

'Allo, *Bertie's Plumbing Service* here. Your pipe problems are our speciality!'

'Oh, good. Hello. I'm Percy. I've got a leak.'

'What's good? Having a leak? True, they're nice with bacon!' Bertie chuckled.

'No, a *leak*, not a leek!' Percy replied with exasperation.

'Just kidding, don't worry. Bathroom or kitchen? Water gushing, is it?' Bertie replied.

'Bathroom. Upstairs. Less gush, more *drip-drip-drip*. Big brown puddle on the floor.'

The line went quiet for a moment.

'I can be there late afternoon. Say four o'clock. Any good?'

A wave of relief washed over Percy.

'Great! The address is 124 Rangoon Road.'

'Right-o! See ya' later.'

The line went dead.

'Have you seen my shoes, Magnus?' asked Percy as he rushed down the stairs.

'By the door,' replied Magnus. 'As usual.'

Percy grabbed them off the rack then squeezed his wet socks into his narrow black shoes.

'Bye! Don't hang around,' grinned Percy, as he grabbed his wizard's cloak and adjusted his pointy hat one last time.

'Never gets old,' Magnus replied with an eyeroll. 'Your shoelaces are undone by the way.'

Percy 'peered' down Rangoon Road. To the average person it looked like any other nice suburban street with tall trees, parked cars and townhouses sandwiched together, but to a wizard, like Percy, who had grown up with dragons as pets, houses that could change shape and walking streetlights, it was refreshingly *dull*. Percy had left all that, and his sister, behind and decided to rent an average house in an average town, much to his magical mirror, Magnus's, annoyance. The one thing Percy couldn't part with was his favourite blue robe pointy hat. Percy took a deep breath of the crisp morning air, opened his squeaky gate and stepped out onto the pavement. Something squelched under his shoe. This was all he needed! He pursed his lips and was wiping whatever it was off his shoe and onto a nearby tuft of grass when the neighbours' front door opened. A woman emerged and walked over to him.

'Morning,' she said, 'I'm Lydia. I've just moved in. Last night, in fact.'

Percy blinked. She had curly ginger hair and the most amazing smile he'd ever seen! *She* wasn't average at all. His brain did somersaults as it tried to get his mouth to utter something.

'Bright,' he stammered.

'Sorry?' Lydia replied in confusion.

'It's bright. Today. In the sky!'

He pointed up.

'Er, yes . . .' she said, increasingly puzzled.

Percy bit his lip and blushed furiously.

'My friend and I . . . we're moving into a tree-house together. I hope we don't fall out.' He grinned.

Lydia cleared her throat.

'It's a joke.' Percy carried on. 'I'm Percy. I'm a wizard!''

Lydia held out her hand.

'Good to meet you Percy the Wizard. I don't suppose you can magic the removal van to arrive, can you? It's late.'

'I'd really like to help,' he said as he looked down at his shoes and remembered what he'd stepped in, 'but I'm actually not great at magic.'

'It was a joke!' smiled Lydia. 'But I do wish they'd get a move on. It's nine forty-five already!'

'Nine forty-five?' Percy exclaimed. 'I'm definitely going to be late. Nice to meet you, Lydia,' he called as he turned and bumped right into the Postman. 'Ooops, sorry, Postie! Got to run, I'm late!'

And with that, Percy ran off down the road.

'But I've got a letter for you, Percy.'

Chapter 2

Cake Date

The gravel crunched under his feet as Percy walked up the wide driveway to the front of the nursing home. He caught his breath and tried to peer through the bay window but it was all steamed up. *They must be serving the tea already*, he thought. He knocked on the huge double doors and a second later, Nurse Jane, with her starched blue uniform and hair tied in a severe bun, opened the door.

'Morning, Percy' she smiled. 'A bit behind schedule, as always, eh! The ladies are waiting for you in the kitchen.'

'A wizard is always late!' he exclaimed proudly,

then frowned. 'No, wait, that's not the right quote.'

'Whatever you say, Percy!' replied Nurse Jane as she ushered him inside. 'Wizard or not, I know that the residents certainly enjoy your wizard costume and your funny tricks.'

Percy was about to correct her and tell her that it wasn't a costume but thought better of it. He straightened his pointy blue hat, swished his cape, and followed her in.

A waft of heat hit him as he entered the kitchen. Everything was polished stainless steel and there were bright lights overhead.

'Percy!' said an old woman with thick glasses, 'here at last! We need you to make your special icing. The buns are ready and waiting.'

'Right you are, Gladys,' said Percy as he rolled up his sleeves. 'Where are Maggie and Agnes today?'

'I'm here!' called Maggie as she emerged from the pantry.

'And I'm here!' said Agnes, and popped her head up from near the sink. 'Morning, Percy!'

Percy grabbed everything he needed to make the icing and walked over to the sideboard. He poured sugar and water into a big bowl and a cloud of fine sugar puffed up, covering his face. He grinned, licked his lips, then stirred the sticky mixture. The three old ladies put three trays of golden buns in front of him.

'Chop the glacé cherries, Maggie, and you get the plates ready, Agnes, love,' said Gladys as Percy poured the icing onto the freshly-baked buns.

In a jiffy, the party of bun-bakers entered the main lounge where the rest of the residents were, slumped in armchairs, TV blaring.

'What's the lovely smell?' said an old man,

rubbing his hands together in anticipation. 'Cake time!'

'And tea o'clock!' said another.

The TV was forgotten. Now it was all about the home-baked buns and tea! All the residents formed an orderly queue while Percy put out the teacups. Then he pulled out his wand and said, '*swish-swash-bimini-bosh!*'

It is a little-known fact among commoners, like you and me, that wizards don't actually need magic words. But Percy thought they sounded good and he knew the old people enjoyed the performance too. Purple sparks fizzed across the row of empty tea cups and each one filled up from the bottom with steamingly strong tea.

Gladys clapped her hands. 'Oooo, I do love it when you do that, Percy dear.'

'I might not be good at other magic, but when it comes to tea, I make a mean magical brew, even if I do say it myself!' Percy smiled.

Nurse Jane picked up a cup, put a dash of milk in and sipped. 'Ah! That you do Percy. Plus I always like it when you use the sparklers with your tricks.

Reminds me of parties and bonfires. Where do you buy them?'

'It isn't a trick. I've told you, I really am a wizard!' Percy replied between bites of bun.

'Of course, of course you are, dear,' said Nurse Jane patting his arm.

Percy shrugged and the nurse went back to her office. No matter what he said or did, she refused to believe him. The old folks were different, though.

'Sparklers indeed!' Gladys nudged him with a smile. 'She can't see magic when it's right in front of her. Though, I must say, we don't often get to meet people like you. Only once in my lifetime have I met another wizard and he was nothing like you. Very snooty he was.'

'Yeah, I've got a sister like that,' said Percy.

'Any chance of a herbal tea with jasmine?' asked an unkempt old man. 'My daughter forgot to bring me some this week.'

'Your wish is my command, sir!' nodded Percy. 'Green tea with jasmine, coming up.'

He waved his wand. '*Swish-swash-bimini-bosh!*' Two green sparks whizzed around each other in a whirlpool shape then burst out in all directions leaving behind the perfect cup of tea. The old man grinned, thanked him and let the next person in the queue step forward.

'Hello, Percy,' said another older chap, 'is it time for a magic show yet? Can you turn Reginald into a toad again?'

Percy held up his hands. 'Oh, Frank, you are a card! I don't think so. Last time we had to call the hairdresser to cut Arnold's six metre nose hair!'

'Oh, come on!' said Frank, 'I know you're bad at magic, but not that bad! What's the worst that could happen? Everyone,' Frank called out, 'time for a magic show. Name your trick!'

The residents cheered and started shouting out requests.

'Rabbit out of the hat. It's a classic.'

'Turn Nurse Jane into a beach ball.'

'Make the lounge into a ball pit.'

'Take us on a field trip to Ice-cream Land!'

Percy looked at Gladys for support but she was clapping her hands together with excitement too.

'Ball pit-ball pit-ball pit!' Frank whipped up the

crowd and all the others began chanting along.

Percy didn't want to disappoint them, so he concentrated on his wand and willed the magic to do his bidding. But instead of brightly-coloured balls, dark green goo bubbled and popped around Reginald's feet. Then, after a flash, Reginald disappeared and in his place was a slimy, warty green toad! It opened its mouth and instead of a croak, Reginald's voice boomed out!

'Why is it always me and the darn toad?'

The Wizard looked apologetically at poor Reginald. Then Frank shuffled over and picked the toad up.

'Ah, my old friend. You always were a grump. Turn him back, Percy, quick before it sticks!'

Percy waved his wand with a wince and Reginald returned to normal, nearly crushing Frank in the process. But then, something even stranger started happening. Both old men began expanding. Blue and green sparks whizzed in all directions. The buttons popped off their shirts. A second later, Frank and Reginald were giant beach balls. Percy's eyes practically popped out of his head! Why could he never get it right? The other residents fell about laughing while the human beach balls bounced around the room whooping and squealing like little boys as they went.

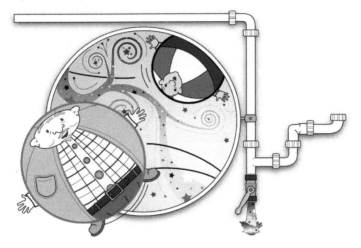

'Watch out!' Frank warned Maggie as he flew through the air.

'I haven't had so much fun in years,' shouted Reginald as he bounced all over the place.

Eventually, but not before the balls had caused quite a mess, a rather red-faced Percy, gathered both of the beach balls up and said, *'swish-swash-bimini-bosh!'* And before he knew it, the pair of old men were grinning and bickering over the last bun.

Phew! Percy flopped down in a chair and sighed, 'that's quite enough magic for now.'

Gladys sat down next to him.

'That was a real show, Percy. The way you pretend to get it wrong always gets a reaction. What are you planning to do after lunch and board games?'

Percy had a nagging feeling he should go home but for the life of him couldn't remember why. Deciding to ignore his wizarding intuition, he said, 'I'm open to suggestions.'

'You could help us in the garden,' said Maggie, 'we need to re-do the rose bed, cut the grass and do some weeding. Maybe you could work your magic on that!'

Percy smiled in agreement, although he had no intention of using magic, not after that morning's magical mishaps! Then, feeling at home, he magicked himself a cup of tea with his finger and took a big slurp.

Chapter 3

About TiMe

After a jolly day at the nursing home, Percy had a delightfully uneventful walk home, until his wand started vibrating urgently as he turned into his road.

Yes, Wand?

'You have a voicemail and four missed calls.' the Wand replied and purple sparks fizzed out of it.

'Why didn't you tell me earlier?' asked Percy, rolling his eyes.

'You asked me to be silent after the beach ball incident. So, do you want to hear your messages or not?' asked the Wand, sounding a little peeved.

'Yes.'

The Wand fizzed and vibrated.

'*Err, Hi. It's Bertie. The Plumber. It's four o'clock and I'm 'ere. Knocked on the door. I can hear someone inside shouting your name. Sounds a trifle miffed. I'll wait in my van and do some paperwork for 10 or 15 minutes or we can rearrange. It sounded urgent this morning. Let me know.* Beeeeep.'

Blast, thought Percy and quickened his pace, his shoes clacking on the pavement.

The Wand fizzed again.

'To listen to the message again, please say *repeat*. To delete this message, please say *delete*. To dial the person back please say *dial*.'

Not now, Wand.

Percy began to jog.

'I'm afraid I don't recognise that request,' the Wand went on, 'to listen to the message again, please say *repeat*. To delete this message, please say *delete*. To dial the person back please say *dial*.'

Percy shoved the Wand in his top pocket. It wasn't far now and he could see a white van parked outside his house. *Yes*, the Plumber was still there.

'Hello!' he called out. 'It's me, Percy, from number 124!'

Bertie stepped out of his van. He was a very tall man and was wearing blue overalls with big black boots. He was carrying a clipboard and had a pencil behind his ear. He was smiling a twinkly smile which went all the way to his friendly brown eyes.

'So *you're* Percy! Whoever Magnus is, he ain't happy with you, mate. I heard a few choice words through the door.'

'Yeah,' Percy puffed, 'he can be a bit like that. Sorry I'm late. I forgot. Volunteering. Nursing home. Distracted.'

'No problem guv'nor.'

'Please. Come. In.'

Percy went up to the door, and opened it with a wave of his wand.

'There you are!' Magnus exclaimed. 'The Plumber came, by the way. You missed him. Oh, and the leak got worse.'

Percy looked up and grimaced. A steady drip hit the hallway floor and a large puddle was starting to form.

'Um, did that mirror just talk?' asked Bertie as he

peered into the hallway.

'What of it?' Magnus replied.

'It did!' Bertie exclaimed. 'Well I never! New technology from Asia, is it?'

Percy picked up the pile of unopened letters from the floor and led the Plumber inside.

'*Technology?*' Magnus narrowed his eyes at Bertie. 'Do I look like a bunch of wires and circuits with fancy blue teeth? I'm an antique! Enchanted. Sophisticated magic I'll have you know, and my name is Magnus. *Tech* indeed.'

Bertie glanced at Percy. The Wizard shrugged.

'Right you are, Magnus. My mistake,' Bertie replied. 'Well, anyway, I'm here to fix that leak so nice to meet you.'

Then Percy and Bertie trudged up the creaky stairs to the bathroom.

'Sorry,' Percy whispered, 'Magnus can come across a bit strong but he's very clever. Does the crossword in minutes.'

'I heard that,' called Magnus from the hall.

'I'm a wizard by the way,' Percy continued, 'though if I'm honest, I'm not very good at magic, although I can magic up an excellent cup of tea.'

'That would explain the wand and the enchanted mirror,' said Bertie. 'I do like a good cuppa and I've never 'ad a magic tea. How's about it, mate? A dash of milk and four sugars sees me right.'

Without thinking, Percy held out his hand and said *'swish-swash-bimini-bosh!'* A white mug appeared at the top of the landing with tea inside. Bertie picked it up and took a slurp.

'Not bad, Percy. But I'm not gonna turn into a frog now, am I?' he chuckled. 'Now, let's see about this leak.'

Bertie stepped into the bathroom, picked up the soaking towel and put his tool box down. Percy stood in the doorway holding his pile of letters.

'See anything?'

'Yeah, found it!' said Bertie and leant under the sink. 'Not surprised you didn't. It's right up the top. A crack in the old cold water pipe. Easy fix.'

Percy sighed with relief and turned his attention to the letters. Bills, more bills and adverts. *Boring.* The last one was a heavy brown envelope. Inside, a wodge of thick paper was folded in two. He pulled it out and flipped the paper open. EVICTION NOTICE was written in bold red letters.

Percy's heart sank as he read on.

Dear Percival Balderham,

This eviction letter is to notify you that you must vacate the leased premises within 21 days from the date of this letter if you fail to pay the overdue rent.

This is in reference to the residential property 124 Rangoon Road, which has transferred legal ownership from Mr Joe Dawson to Ms Drusilla Balderham. You currently owe £1,343.16 in overdue rent dating back 4 months. The new legal owner does not wish to extend the deadline for overdue rent any further. The current tenancy agreement expires in 6 months and will not be renewed.

Failure to comply with this eviction notice or pay overdue rent will result in legal action against you. For further details please contact the legal representative of Ms. Drusilla Balderham via letter to 34b Lawyer Court, Hawksmoor Street, London, W1 3TR.

Sincerely,

Joe Dawson

Ps. Sorry, mate. You were a good tenant and I know we'd talked about you buying 124 Rangoon Road in a couple of years but she gave an offer I couldn't refuse. All the best. J.

Drusilla! What does my sister want with this house and why does she always ruin everything? thought Percy.

'You OK?' Bertie asked. 'You look like you've seen a ghost.'

'My sister has just bought this house from my landlord and she wants to kick me out if I don't pay the overdue rent. She's doing it to punish me. She thinks I'm a coward for leaving the Wizarding Community and trying to live a normal life, like a commoner. She wants me to run home to Mother with my tail between my legs.'

'Ah,' said Bertie, 'families can be complicated whether you're a wizard or a commoner, mate. I've got an uncle like that. Never happy unless someone is having trouble. Bertie quietly packed up his tools.

'One bit of good news, though,' said Bertie as he packed up his tools, 'the leak is fixed.'

Percy smiled but it didn't reach his eyes.

'Thanks. How much do I owe you?'

Bertie looked at his clipboard.

'That's 55 quid.'

Percy nodded, disappeared for a moment, then came back with a glass jar. Inside four pound coins rattled.

'This isn't enough is it?' he said.

Bertie scratched his head then slurped the last bit of his drink.

'I tell you what, that was a good tea. A tea worth twenty seven pounds and fifty pence I'd say. Make me another and we're even. I need to sort out junk in the back of my van so I could use some fuel.'

Percy looked over at Bertie.

'Really?' He asked.

'Are you joking?' The Plumber replied. 'It's at least two hours until dinner time. My stomach will be grumbling if I don't have a cuppa soon! Come on. Let's go down to my van. You can tell me all about this sister of yours.'

Percy fell into step with Bertie and the pair passed Magnus on their way out. The Mirror was frowning in concentration. On the other side of the hallway a newspaper was perched on an easel.

'Oi, you two. Out of the way. Oh, actually, who was the egyptian god of cats? Six letters.'

'Bastet,' Bertie replied quickly.

'Not just a plumber after all, eh?' the Mirror grinned.

When Bertie opened the back of his van, Percy had to hold his mouth shut. It was messier than his bedroom floor before wash day! Copper pipes, plastic joints, wrenches and other tools were heaped together like a real-life game of pick-up sticks! Bertie looked back at the Wizard.

'Yeah, I know. A bit of pickle. Right hold this.'

'I'll help you sort it out,' said Percy.

'What quick-like, with magic you mean?' Bertie replied hopefully.

Percy winced.

'Just my hands if that's OK. I'd probably turn the pipes into snakes or melt the copper into ingots if I used magic.'

'Ah, fair enough. Let's get started.'

Together, they piled the plastic poles and pipes, stacked the spare loo seats and organised the spanners, in companionable silence. It took no time at all and when they were finished, Percy swished his wand and they both enjoyed a brew perched on the lip of the van.

'I've got an idea,' said Bertie, 'you need money and I need help, so why don't you join me on a few jobs tomorrow? If you could pay that rent in time, then at least you could stay at your place until the end of the lease.'

'Learn to be a plumber you mean, like you?' Percy replied hopefully.

'Yeah, why not? You can be my apprentice,' said Bertie, 'especially with that magic tea of yours.'

Percy shook Bertie's hand and grinned from ear to ear. Maybe his sister wouldn't ruin his plans for a normal life after all.

Chapter 4

New Starter

Bong!

Percy heard his grandfather clock chiming the hour from the floor below. He stretched and rolled out of bed.

'I'm up,' he called. Then he sniffed the nearest pair of black socks. *Still got another day in them*, he thought. Then, after pulling his robe over his head, a waft of onions hit him. He pulled the armpit closer then wrinkled his nose.

'That's a *wrong pong*. I need a shower,' he muttered.

In his pants, vest and socks he shuffled down the landing, the floorboards creaking under the thin carpet.

'You're up early!' said Magnus. 'What time is it?'

'seven o'clock, by my reckoning and tea o'clock too,' Percy replied cheerfully.

'Grandfather Clock, is he right?' called Magnus.

'It's two minutes past seven,' the Clock replied.

'And what time did Percy set the alarm for?' Magnus asked curiously.

'five o'clock and not a minute after!' said the Clock. 'Which means Percy's late. Again! No wait, I've been tricked.'

Percy opened the bathroom door and basked in the early morning sunshine. He was feeling rather pleased with himself, what with having a job to go to and all. He'd show Drusilla that she couldn't beat him. After turning on the shower, he brushed his teeth, then decided to put all of his clothes in the washing basket but it was full already! *Must be wash day*, he thought. Pulling back the shower curtain he tested the water and snatched his hand back – it was freezing!

'Hotter,' he said involuntarily whilst holding his wand and suddenly the room filled with steam like a jungle, except that there were green sparks whizzing in arcs through the mist. Accidental magic was a sure sign of a wizard.

'Not *that* hot!' he said in frustration. 'I just want a warm shower!'

And sure enough, outside, while the sun shone, a warm rain shower started! Percy put his wand down, closed his eyes and took a deep breath. That wasn't what he wanted at all! *Be patient with yourself*, he thought, repeating the words his magic teacher had taught him in wizarding school, *magic is a tool like any other*. Then in a calm voice he expressed his will.

'I would like a warm shower inside this bathroom . . . from that shower head . . . using the water from the boiler downstairs . . . Please!' said Percy.

Seconds later, some steam was accompanied by a rush of lovely warm water from the shower.

Showered, dressed and clean, Percy trooped down the stairs carrying his laundry. On route to the kitchen, he flipped the crossword book onto the next page.

'Much obliged,' said Magnus.

Then, Percy bundled the dirty clothes into the washing machine, added the powder and switched it on. He quickly scoffed some breakfast and when Bertie honked his horn bang on eight o'clock, Percy was ready for his first day as a plumber's apprentice. He polished off the last bite of crumpet, shifted his pointy hat and marched down the hallway.

'Good luck!' Magnus called.

'Thanks!' smiled Percy as he left.

At the very same moment, his new neighbour, Lydia, emerged from her house carrying a rubbish bag.

'Good morning, Percy.'

The Wizard stopped dead in his tracks. *Say something*, he urged himself. 'I went to buy some camouflage trousers the other day, but I couldn't find any.'

'Another joke?' Lydia asked.

Percy nodded and smiled just as Bertie tooted his

horn again. Then he pointed at the van.

'Got to go. Bye.'

'Morning, mate. We've got a nice job today – a real goodun'!'

'Morning,' said Percy as he pulled off his pointy hat, clambered inside and put his seat belt on.

'So, Mr Wizard, who's the girl?' Bertie chuckled then revved his engine and pulled out into the road.

'Lydia. She just moved in,' Percy replied.

'Looks like a nice lass.'

'Yeah, she is,' Percy replied dreamily.

'We're off to the public swimming pool today. Some sort of leak. Strange story though,' began Bertie.

Percy watched the world go by as the van zipped through the traffic, while Bertie chatted away in the background, but Percy's mind was on Lydia.

'Hey, you listening?' said Bertie and tapped the dashboard in front of Percy.

Percy blinked.

'Sorry. What was the story?'

'We're there, I'll explain everything in a bit. You

go and get my tools and a spare pair of overalls. Don't want your robe getting dirty.'

Percy followed Bertie's instructions, then joined him at the entrance to the pool. A big sign hung across the double doors; *Closed for repair*. Percy caught a whiff of the tangy chlorine smell coming from inside as Bertie pulled the handle. A young woman greeted them from behind the reception desk.

'Hello, I take it you're the Plumber?'

Bertie nodded.

'Who's the guy with the blue pointy hat, then? Your *magical* assistant?'

Bertie cleared his throat.

'This is Percy, my apprentice, and yes, he is a wizard, if you have a problem with that, we'll go. And I'd appreciate it if you treated him with the respect he deserves from now on,' Bertie retorted, irritated by the young woman's joke.

'Look, sorry,' she replied. 'I'm a bit stressed. If I can't get this problem sorted, my manager will fire me.'

'Right you are, then, we'd better get to work,'

said Bertie and patted Percy's shoulder.

'Like I explained on the phone,' said the young woman as she showed them building blueprints, which were laid out on the reception desk, 'every night for the last week half the water in the main pool just disappears. Every morning we have to top it up again. But this morning was different. It was still full when we got here, but the water was really, really warm. We've checked the main pump and the water heater and we can't find anything wrong except that the temperature dial was turned up and none of the staff did it. It's a total mystery!'

'That it is!' said Bertie scratching his chin. 'We'd better get to work, Percy. Come on, follow me.'

They walked into the maintenance area, which had thick metal pipes criss-crossed over the breeze-block walls and the ceiling too. Then they turned left into the pump room, which was dimly lit and filled with the low hum of the pump. Bertie had a good look at it, shining his torch so that he could see properly. But after a while, he turned to Percy and shrugged. He couldn't see anything wrong with it.

'I'm going to take a look at the pipes at the back,'

said Bertie. 'Could you go and check the filters in the pool, please Percy? Just put your hand in the water near one of the grates, you'll feel the current if it's working.'

Percy nodded and off he went. His footsteps echoed off the high ceiling and the large windows. The pool was full. In fact, it was too full and water was all over the tiles around the pool. He put the toolbox down then glanced at the water. He could have sworn he saw it ripple back, as if it was saying 'hello'. When he put his hand near the filter, he could feel the current sucking the water down through a grate. So it wasn't the filter, then. But just then, something touched his wrist.

Percy leapt back!

He screamed.

Bertie came running.

'What's going on, Percy?'
'I . . . I . . . I'm not sure,' Percy stammered, 'but

I could have sworn that something just touched me but there's nothing there!'

'Okaaaaay,' Bertie said, at a loss for anything else to say.

'But the pump *is* working,' said Percy, trying to act normal.

'I checked the heater and that's working fine too,' said Bertie. 'It was a bit hotter than normal so I turned it down. I'm a bit stumped as to what to do next, everything seems to be working just fine. This really is a bit of a mystery.'

'*Hmph!*'

'Did you hear that?' said Bertie.

Percy nodded, then frowned and poked the water with his finger. 'Maybe the echo?'

'*Hmph!*'

'There it is again,' said Bertie, 'something very strange is happening here. You stay here and I'll go and check the water outflow.'

Left alone again, Percy's wizarding senses started tingling. Something magical was afoot, he was sure of it, but what?

Then the water rippled again.

Percy nearly jumped out of his skin.

'Don't panic!' said a voice from the water, 'I won't bite, I promise! You're a wizard, aren't you? Unless that outfit is a costume.'

And then, the water rose up into two tendrils and waved!

'Well, I *am* a wizard,' said a rather flabbergasted Percy, 'but that's beside the point, 'the question is, 'who are you?''

'Oh, I figured you'd know if you have magic in your blood,' said the voice, then the water swirled and twisted into a long snake-like body with skinny legs like a frog and a head like a crocodile. 'I'm a water dragon. Earl is the name. Liquid is my game.'

'Good to meet you, I guess,' replied Percy and raised his eyebrows. 'I'm Percy.'

'Likewise,' said Earl with a watery smile. 'I'm glad you're here actually. I'm in a bit of a fix. I was going to leave before the Commoners got here but my bath was so warm and I fell asleep. They've closed off the pipe that adds fresh water to the pool, which was how I got in, and now I can't get out.'

'I'm sure we can come up with something,' said

Percy, wracking his brains for a solution. 'And knowing you're here also solves part of the mystery – your body is displacing the water and making it spill over the edge of the pool and into the pipes. Wait, can't you leave through the outflow pipe?'

'You mean go to the commoner sewer? I'd rather not.'

On reflection, Percy agreed. That didn't sound nice at all. He would have to come up with another idea but, before he could, Bertie walked in. He was looking at his clipboard and scratching his head.

'Funny thing Percy,' he said, 'the sluice gate on the outflow is wide open but the water just stops like there is an invisible barrier. I just don't get it. There's something strange going on here.'

Then the Plumber looked up. His mouth fell open and his clipboard clattered to the floor.

'What the . . .'

'Bertie, don't panic,' called Percy, 'it's a . . .'

'Hi, I'm Earl,' the Dragon interrupted. A tendril of water picked up the clipboard and passed it back to Bertie. 'You dropped this.'

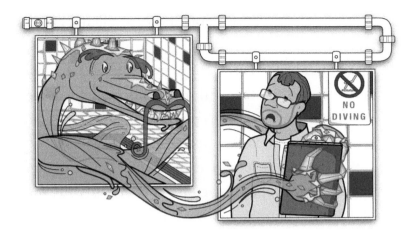

Bertie took the clipboard but couldn't take his eyes off the Dragon.

'Percy. I need a tea. A strong tea.'

'Coming right up, Boss,' said Percy as he raced over, swished his wand in the air and magicked up a much-needed cuppa for the perplexed plumber. 'I have an idea for fixing this and I think we should keep it to ourselves − in my experience the more magic involved, the more trouble there is, and I don't want Earl here getting into trouble.'

Bertie took a gulp of tea, eyes still wide, then glanced at Percy.

'I like a good oolong tea myself,' said Earl.'

'Er, that's a water dragon and he is talking about tea,' spluttered Bertie.

'Yes,' replied Percy, thinking that it was all perfectly within the realms of normality, before quickly moving on to his plan. 'See those tube-like floats? I have an idea. I just need you to . . .'

But before he could explain, the door swung open. The receptionist came rushing in with the blueprint. Then she spotted Earl and stopped dead in her tracks.

'Good morning, Commoner,' he grinned.

She screamed, then sagged to the floor in a heap.

Chapter 5

Turning the Tide

'Drat!' Percy said to himself, then ran over to check she was OK.

Phew, just fainted, he thought. It was now or never. They needed to sort all this out before she came round.

'Bertie, take a tube float and jam it in the outflow. Where is the inflow control?'

The Plumber picked up the lilac float and pointed back to the pump room.

'Sorry to cause such trouble,' said Earl. 'But it really was a very nice bath. Anything I can do to help?'

Percy smiled at the Dragon.

'Just be ready to go on your way as soon as I open the valve.'

Over in the pump room, Percy quickly found the control and flipped the switch. The sound of rushing water added to the hum of the pump. Gently closing the door, he went back into the main pool, where he found Bertie was helping the Receptionist assistant, to her feet. *Play it cool*, thought Percy, and walked towards them. Then, after a large gulp of tea and noisily clearing his throat, Bertie spoke, 'so my apprentice here has done me proud. He's found the problem, haven't you Percy?'

The Receptionist looked confused. 'B . . . b . . . but I'm sure I saw a monster in the water! And my head is sore. I think I bumped my head?'

'You just tripped on something,' Percy said, a little too loudly. 'Nasty. Hazard of the business. But, as Bertie said, we've found the problem. One of your floats was jammed in the outflow. Twisted right up, it was. Hard to spot. We can show you.'

The Receptionist followed them to the outflow and saw the float that Bertie had just planted.

'That's odd,' she frowned, 'I wonder how it got through the filter.'

Bertie stepped over and winked at Percy.

'Well, that's the funny thing,' said Bertie, tapping his clipboard, 'I didn't need the keys you gave me because the door wasn't locked. I wonder if one of the children did it as a prank? You know how kids can be!'

'That does make sense, I guess,' she replied. 'My manager would think I'm nuts if I told him a monster did it! Thanks, and just send the bill over and I'll get it paid.'

Just then, Bertie's phone rang. 'Another job,' he said and smiled at the Receptionist, 'come on, Percy.'

Bertie and Percy sat in the van and ate their cheese & pickle sandwiches with gusto. It was well past lunchtime. Percy was thinking about all the practical tips Bertie had given him during their second job that day, which they'd only just finished. *Fitting a new*

bathtub was surprisingly complicated, Percy concluded. His thoughts were interrupted by Bertie's phone ringing.

'Allo, Bertie's Plumbing Service here. Your pipe problems are our speciality! Oh, yeah, the nursing home. Broken toilet. Righto. We'll be there in a jiffy. Just polishing off our lunch. I'll have my apprentice, Percy, with me. The Wizard? Yeah, the one and the same. Brilliant. Yep. Goodbye.'

Bertie popped the last bit of sandwich in his mouth and started the engine.

After a quick cruise across town, they pulled into the gravel driveway. Percy hopped out and got the tools, while Bertie made some notes on his clipboard. Nurse Jane met them at the door and ushered them inside.

'I didn't know you were a plumber, Percy,' she said.

'Just started today,' he smiled.

'This way,' said Nurse Jane and led them upstairs. 'A certain gentleman has some explaining to do!'

On the landing stood a rather sheepish-looking

Frank with a broken loo handle in his hand!

'Hi, Percy! Who's your friend?' asked Gladys, popping her head round the door.

'Hi, Gladys. This is Bertie, my new boss. He is a plumber. We've come to sort out the broken loo.'

Nurse Jane returned to her office, leaving Bertie and Percy to fix the loo. Meanwhile, Frank snuck back in.

'Psssst! Percy,' he hissed. 'Percy.'

'Yes, Frank, what is it?'

The old man put his fingers to his lips. 'Alright, I'll talk straight. I blocked the loo with a *bigger-than-normal* number two – overdid it with those delicious buns this morning! Too many of them I reckon. I tried everything! Coathangers, more toilet paper, you name it. I panicked and pumped the handle a bit hard. Came off in my hand, it did! The trouble is, I don't want Gladys to know. I'm a bit sweet on her and it might put her off!'

Percy stifled a grin while Bertie gave a chuckle.

'Don't worry, Frank,' said Percy, 'your secret is safe with me.'

After fixing the new handle, the three of them went back downstairs to Nurse Jane's office.

'All fixed,' said Bertie, 'faulty handle by the looks of it,'

He winked at Frank.

'I see. Well, thank you for helping us at such short notice.'

Just then, Gladys came through with a tray of iced buns, an empty teapot and teacups.

'Anyone fancy a cake?'

Frank swallowed, looked at Percy and blushed.

'Of course, Gladys. I never say no to your cooking.'

Chapter 6

A Spell of Bother

The next morning Percy was full of beans. Having regaled Magnus with yesterday's successes, eaten breakfast and brushed his teeth, he was now standing on the pavement outside his house, eagerly awaiting Bertie. He couldn't wait to get cracking on that day's jobs. But Bertie was late. It was a little chilly in the wind so he pulled his robe tighter under his plumber's overalls. As he looked up and down the road again, hoping he would see Bertie's van approaching, his neighbour, Lydia, emerged from her house.

'Percy! Oh, thank goodness. You're a plumber, aren't you?'

The Wizard moved his lips but no words came out.

'It's just that I've got a dripping tap in my bathroom and it's driving me nuts when I'm trying to sleep.'

'I could take a look, for you,' Percy finally said.

Lydia's grateful smile sent him weak at the knees so he was glad to hear the hoot of Bertie's van – he had back up! The van pulled up with a skid and out jumped Bertie.

'Sorry! Overslept. Hi, there. You're Lydia aren't you? Percy mentioned he had a new neighbour.'

'He did?' Lydia looked across at the Wizard as his cheeks reddened. 'He was just about to help me with a dripping tap. Can he still do it before you whisk him off to work?'

Bertie made a big show of looking at his watch then winked at Percy.

'I think we can squeeze you in. Show us the problem. Percy, grab the tools.'

In the modern white bathroom, Bertie and Percy quickly got to work.

'So are you really a wizard?'

'I sure am,' replied Percy as he fiddled at the back of the sink. 'I'm not great at magic though – except tea. I'm really good at magicking up tea!'

'Yup, brilliant at tea, he is,' Bertie confirmed.

'So you can't use magic to fix the tap, then?' asked Lydia.

But Percy was concentrating too hard to pay any attention to the question. He gave a final twist on the spanner.

'I think that's done it!' he said.

Everyone watched in suspense. Then, right on time, another drip sploshed into the sink.

'Oh,' signed Percy.

'I think the seal has gone,' said Bertie. 'I don't think I've got a spare so I'll need to order it. Could save some time if you use magic just this one, mate.'

'It's not a good idea, trust me!' said Percy and held up his hands.

'Oh, go on. For me?' pleaded Lydia and smiled her annoyingly nice smile.

Percy couldn't say no now, so he pulled out his wand and rolled up his sleeves.

'Here goes,' said Percy rather nervously.

After a moment of quiet, Bertie looked over at the tap.

'No sparks,' he said.

A loud thud came from behind the shower curtain. Then something moved behind it. Something BIG. And this was closely followed by a VERY strange noise – something between a bark and wail. Lydia went white, her eyes wide with fright. Bertie froze. Percy bravely pulled back the shower curtain. His stomach sank into his boots. He'd done it again.

There, lying on its back, was an enormous seal! The tap stopped dripping but no-one noticed.

'Blimey!' Bertie exclaimed. 'That's not quite the kind of seal I had in mind!'

Lydia said nothing and was backing slowly out of the room.

'Right you are,' said Bertie, 'I think maybe

we ask the seal to go back to the ocean, don't you, Percy?'

The Wizard sat on the loo seat and put his head in his hands. Why couldn't he get it right, just once? And all the while the seal was clapping his flippers and barking. Without looking at him, Percy swished his finger and the seal disappeared. It had worked, for once, but that didn't make him feel any better. He really hoped he would be a better plumber than he was a wizard.

Bertie put his hand on Percy's shoulder. 'That was one classy trick. Pretty funny when you think about it. And look, the drip stopped as well.'

'Lydia, the tap is fixed and the. er, seal is gone,' Bertie called.

'Thank you,' Lydia's muffled reply came through her bedroom door. 'I'll just be in here for a moment if you don't mind.'

'Righto, we'll see ourselves out. Got a busy day today and all that,' Bertie replied and tugged his friend up.

At least the day couldn't get worse, thought Percy as he followed Bertie to the van.

Chapter 7

Judgemental Juncture

Percy sat in silence during the journey to the next job. He kept playing the scene over and over in his mind. Each second a painful and embarrassing spike.

'We're here,' said Bertie. 'Tools like usual. Now, before we go in there, I think I'd better tell you something.'

Oh-no, Percy thought, *I've disappointed another person. Or am I going to get fired?*

'This client,' Bertie began, 'well, he's a bit, well,

stiff. I've been fitting a kitchen for him but the sink he ordered was a posh one so it's only just arrived and it's been three weeks. Just don't expect any smiles or chit-chat and leave the talking to me.'

Percy relaxed. *Phew*. It wasn't him.

Percy closed the small gate behind him and noted the sea of white pebbles peppered with small, completely spherical, bushes. Snaking through them, a line of metal arched up and around like a rollercoaster. *Very-very modern*, Percy thought. The gleaming black front door opened soundlessly before Bertie even knocked and a short middle-aged man, dressed in a grey suit with highly-polished grey shoes, stood waiting for them. Across his forehead was a frown as deep as a valley. He greeted them with a tut.

'Good morning, Mr Windthrup,' Bertie said cheerfully.

'You're late.'

'Bad traffic. This is my apprentice, Percival Balderham. Percy for short. The sink you ordered is finally in, so once we get that installed, the job's finished.'

'About time,' muttered Mr Windthrup as he shuffled back into the house. 'Plastic bags on your feet. I don't want your dirty clomping plumbing boots marking my new cream carpet. Oh, and I'm working from home today so keep the noise down. No chit chat. Fix the sink and leave. I'll transfer the remaining amount owed if I'm happy with the job.'

Bertie raised an eyebrow in Percy's direction then shrugged. Percy carefully did as he was instructed, holding onto his pointy hat all the while.

'Lovely place, you've got. Very neat,' said Percy, determined to make a good impression.

'Lovely! Neat!' said Mr Windthrup almost spitting the words back. 'This house is a work of art. As if someone like you would know anyway. And what's with the pointy hat? You're not a wizard are you?'

'Magicks a great cuppa if you'd like one?' Bertie interrupted to try to diffuse the rather terse exchange. But it was no good.

'I am,' said Percy.

But his friendly smile was met by a glare from Mr Windthrup.

'Magic is a sham,' their grumpy client replied.

'I've had dealings with your kind before. Pompous tricksters, the lot of them. I wasn't good enough for one of your schools, yet here I am *without* magic and the richest man in town. Lovely, neat! Pah. Just the kind of condescending thing a wizard would say.'

Bertie cleared his throat loudly. 'We'll be carrying on with the job now, Mr Windthrup.'

Percy crept into the kitchen wordlessly and placed down the tool box. He felt a little ball of angry fire in his belly and he pictured Mr Windthrup's upturned nose. *Why are people so prejudiced? He doesn't even know me*, he thought as he loudly plonked the set of spanners on the granite worktop.

'Easy now,' Bertie whispered with a grin. 'And watch out for that gold ring, there.'

'Sorry,' said Percy, 'I couldn't help it. He was so horrid!'

'You have to take the good with the bad in this line of work, mate,' said Bertie reassured. 'Plus, I charged triple. *Hazard pay* for having to deal with his rudeness.'

After a brief explanation of what they needed

to do, Bertie and Percy went out to the van to get the sink. After a lot of puffing, heaving, tipping and turning, they lowered it into position with a gentle clunk.

'Careful! I heard that,' Mr Windthrup shouted from the other room.

Bertie rolled his eyes.

'Now, Percy, get the sealant and squeeze it around the edge while I lift up the sink.'

Next, under instruction from Bertie, Percy fitted the water outflow and tightened the joints. Then he waited nervously as Bertie inspected the work. Bertie sucked his teeth and sighed.

'Just a few things I need to do to make this right,' said Bertie. 'Then I'll fit the taps. You clean up while I'm doing that and then we can be off.'

Percy felt Bertie's disappointment keenly and tried to be quiet as he put the tools away and swept up their mess.

Just as they were getting ready to go, with the taps fitted and all Percy's little mistakes fixed, Mr Windthrup barged past them and stood in the middle of his immaculate kitchen.

'I assume by all of the *loud* rustling you're finished,' he said.

'Yep,' Bertie replied. 'All done and the bill's on the side.'

Mr Windthrup walked over to the sink. 'That sealant doesn't look straight and is that a chip on my worktop? I shall inspect everything and make deductions from your bill for any imperfections or damage to my property,' said Mr Windthrup in his mean, prissy voice.

Percy was furious. His anger built up like a pressure cooker. *Why did people have to be so unpleasant?* Bertie was furious too but could tell that they needed to get out of there before his young apprentice did something they would both regret. Without another word, while making a mental note to never work for Mr Windthrup again, Bertie picked up their kit and led Percy out of the house.

Percy stomped to the back of the van but when he couldn't open the door, without warning, his frustration bubbled over. Red sparks whizzed and fizzed in a great chaotic cloud that blew the door clean off his hinges with a gigantic bang!

'What's happened?' Bertie called out in concern.

'Oh, nothing,' snapped Percy. '*Repair now!*'

He swished his finger and the door flew up into the air and clipped itself back into place. Maybe he was getting better at magic! Then he slung the tools in the back of the van and got in the passenger side. Bertie shook his head and turned on the engine.

The pair sat in silence on the drive to 124 Rangoon Road. By the time they arrived at Percy's house, his anger and frustration had turned into a mixture of confusion and nervousness.

'How come we're here? Are you firing me because of all the mistakes today?' he asked.

'Nothing like that, honest,' said Bertie and tried to reassure him. 'I've got some things I need to do this afternoon. I'll be in contact about our next job in a couple of days.'

'Oh, OK,' said Percy but he couldn't help but notice that Bertie had not made eye contact when he said this, 'bye then.'

Bertie drove off, waving cheerfully and Percy trudged up to his front door and walked inside. He was feeling very down in the dumps. Today had been a disaster, even though some magic had actually gone to plan!

'You're back early! Been sacked already, have you?' said Magnus but his joke fell flat. 'Now you're here, can you turn the page on my crossword book?'

Percy sighed and walked past without stopping.

'Percy?' Magnus said with an edge of concern. 'What's happened? Did you get yourself in trouble?'

'I don't want to talk about it, Magnus,' Percy muttered as he went up the stairs and flopped on his bed.

Percy closed his eyes to shut out the world but sleep didn't come. He just lay there as the minutes turned into hours and tried to ignore the rumbling in his tummy.

'Go away,' he said to himself but it kept on rumbling.

Resigned, he got up and went to the kitchen. After putting two pieces of bread in the toaster he looked out of the window. It was early evening now and the sun was dipping in the sky. He'd always liked twilight. That in-between space. Maybe he'd go for a walk this evening. But his thoughts – and his snack — were interrupted by a loud knock at the door.

Whoever it was banged again.

'Open up!'

Percy nervously unlocked the door . . .

Chapter 8

A Long Stretch

'Wizard Percival Balderham?' said an unpleasantly stern-looking woman. 'We are officers of the Justice and Magic Inspectorate, better known as the J.M.I. You are under arrest for breaking the Wizarding Code.'

'Percy, run!' shouted Magnus.

'But I haven't done anything wrong,' replied a bewildered Percy as three J.M.I. officers shouldered through the door and pushed their way into his home. All were wearing pointy blue hats, heavy dark blue robes and matching frowns.

'You do not have to say anything, but it will

probably harm your defence if you do not mention, when questioned, something you later rely on in Wizarding Court. You will surrender your wand and hat, and accompany us to *Noo-gnar*. NOW!'

Not Noo-gnar, surely? thought Percy as a shiver ran down his spine. *Noo-gar* was the stuff of every wizard's nightmares. It was the horrifying magical detention dungeon, a maze of cells in the basement of the J.M.I. headquarters. And every magical being knew that once you were locked up in *Noo-gar*, that was it! Percy had never heard of anyone ever getting out. Innocence didn't matter in *Noo-gnar*.

'But wait,' Percy pleaded. 'Please. What did I do?'

'Shut up Percy,' Magnus hissed, 'don't say anything. Ever. Trust me!'

'Come on, Maud,' one of the other officers moaned, 'this is the last one before we knock off and go to *The Drunken Duck* for a drink.'

'What you did or didn't do is not a matter for us, you little weasel,' Officer Maud explained nastily, 'it's for the Wizarding Court to decide. We don't want a scene. Not good for public relations, so just do what you're told.'

Then she snatched his wand from his top pocket and pulled his hat off. The other two officers hauled him up and dragged him outside.

'Not a word, Percy!' Magnus shouted after him desperately. 'Keep it zipped!'

A distant bell tolled and Percy marked another white line on the wall next to his bed. Twenty lines in all. Twenty days in the *Noo-gnar* dungeon. And he still hadn't been told what his supposed crime was. Twenty days and not a peep from the J.M.I. officers or anyone else. Percy had grown used to the constant pit of anxiety in his stomach. Would this be his life now? Should he have fought more to evade the officers?

He looked up. There was no window in his miserable cell. The only light came from an orb hanging from the ceiling. Its orange glow cast shadows across the bare cell, which was only five paces across. It had a stone bench at the back that doubled as a bed and a small bucket in the corner was his loo. The walls were made of huge stone blocks with mortar filling in any cracks. The thick iron door had a single peephole so his gaolers could spy on him but it didn't work the other way. And next to the door were two metal hatches through which his food was delivered. There was nothing to do but Percy had kept himself busy by weaving and plaiting fresh straw into a thin mattress for his bed, then he'd done a lid for the bucket and finally a mat for the floor, until there was no straw left.

Using his plumber's overalls as a pillow, he lay down. There was nothing else to do. He could hear the rain outside. At first he thought it was strange to hear rain in a dungeon but then he remembered *Noo-gnar* was underneath the Justice & Magic Inspectorate headquarters, which was a floating island! It was said that it only moved when the Chief Justice Wizard fancied a better view from his bedchamber and it was currently parked next to some famous mountain range. *Oh how I long to feel the rain on my cheeks or the wind whistling by*, Percy thought.

His thoughts were suddenly interrupted by both food hatches opening at once. Two trays were pushed through the slots. On one was a steaming heap of creamy mashed potato and sausages. On the other was a bowl of what could only be called thin soup. Grease and brown lumps floated on the top. Each tray had a label with a spidery written message on it. The nice food plaque said, *eat this lovely meal, you deserve it and you can have more. By doing so you'll confirm what we know already, you're guilty. Then we can all move on.* The other label said, *if you're so sure you're innocent, you won't mind eating this slop. By doing so, you'll confirm what we know already, you're close to confessing your guilt.* Percy's mouth watered as he looked at the sausages – he really LOVED sausages – but he resisted. He pushed the nice food back through the hatch and settled for his twentieth bowl of brown broth.

After wolfing it down, Percy heard something he hadn't heard before. It was a scratching noise and it was coming from the other side of the left wall. Percy raised an eyebrow and got down on all fours. The scratching got louder and was followed by some very deliberate taps. Then, suddenly, the iron door screeched on its hinges. A hunched-over gaoler with a droopy eye held up a lamp and peered at Percy. He gave a toothless grin when he saw the Wizard on the floor like a dog.

'Going mad already? Young people. No stamina. Come on. Your presence is requested by the Chief Justice Wizard himself. Done a bad thing no doubt. Must be up for initial sentencing. Only the guilty in *Noo-gnar*, they say.'

He waved the lamp to encourage Percy out of his cell.

'Sentencing? You mean I'm going to be told what my punishment will be. I don't even know why I'm in here!' Percy replied.

'Me neither. Just a gaoler. Serving m'own sentence.'

'What did you do?' Percy asked as he dusted off his hands.

'Stole a dragon's treasure. Dragon didn't fancy

eatin' me so the J.M.I. made me serve as a gaoler. I'm here until I get a dragon's forgiveness. Long while ago now. Well, you know dragons. They hold a grudge.'

Despite his own unfortunate circumstances Percy couldn't help but feel sorry for him.

'My name is Percy. What's yours?'

'My name? It's been a long time since I had a name,' the Gaoler looked down and frowned as he tried to remember. 'Henry, yes, that was it.' The Gaoler smiled to himself for a split second. 'Come on, Percy. I've got to escort you otherwise they'll send the Griffin down to check and we don't want that, trust me.'

Percy nodded and followed Henry down the corridor. Like the cells, the thick stone rose up into a lofty darkness only broken up by dimly glowing orbs. Either side, more cells held inmates. They went up two flights of stone steps and they were above ground. Percy drank in the fresh air and the natural light. Through another door, they passed another two rows of cells, but this time only iron bars held back the inmates, and there were windows and wooden furniture. Percy walked by fairies, witches, gnomes, elves and other magical creatures. All of them with their heads bowed as if they were under orders not to look up.

'This lot are minor offences,' Henry explained, 'they'll be out in a week.'

What have I done to deserve being in Noo-gnar? Percy thought for the thousandth time.

Two J.M.I. officers opened the next panelled door and grabbed his elbows.

'See you later,' called Henry, 'good luck! You'll need it.'

Chapter 9

Judgement Hour

Percy gulped as he entered the main court. As tall as it was wide and everything was polished hardwood and brass. The seats had red cushions and it was lit by splendid chandeliers. He looked down at his soiled blue robes and felt very out of place. In front of him, a witch and a gargoyle sat on raised podiums with a third seat empty in the middle. *The Judges*, Percy thought and craned his neck to look up at them. Both wore pointy grey hats and long white judicial robes and both looked extremely forbidding. The Witch, Judge Primrose, looked down her long knobbly nose at him, while the Gargoyle, Judge Mudd, a bored look on his face, fiddled with some papers. The two officers pushed Percy into the dock and told him to sit. Strangers filed into the public gallery. Then the Jurors took their seats. The Jury was made up of a mixture of magical creatures with a few commoners thrown in for good measure. And when everyone was in position, a door behind the podiums creaked open and the third, and chief judge entered the courtroom.

'Chief Justice Wizard. All rise,' a clerk called out.

The Wizard glared down at everyone like an

angry owl. And just then, Percy recognised him. It was his old school teacher, *Mr Ingram*.

'Ah, the Percival Balderham case. I've been looking forward to this. I always knew you'd amount to nothing. Do you remember me, boy?' the Judge narrowed his eyes.

'I do, Mr Ingram,' replied Percy.

'You will address me by my rank, boy. It's *Chief Justice Wizard Ingram*.'

'Yes, Chief Justice Wizard Ingram. Please may I know why I am on trial?' Percy asked.

'Impertinent Wizard! We are the ones who ask the questions, not you!' Judge Mudd growled.

Judge Ingram cleared his throat.

'Indeed. On this occasion, however, I'll make an exception. You stand accused *and guilty* of theft from a lowly commoner no less, and of bringing the Wizarding community into disrepute. A grave offence given your magical abilities.'

'Who?'

The question burst from Percy's lips. Everyone gasped in the courtroom. He even shocked himself. The red-faced Judge flared his nostrils and touched his wand to the podium. A loud *BANG* silenced the room.

'Order! Do you plead guilty or not guilty?'

'I'm not a thief!' said Percy. 'Not guilty, Your Honour, Chief Justice Wizard Ingram.'

'A guilty wizard who pleads not guilty? How novel,' said the Witch Judge in a high shrill voice while the Gargoyle Judge growled and shuffled in his seat and a chorus of gasps was heard from the gallery.

Judge Ingram banged his wand again and the room went quiet.

'I had hoped to have a quick guilty verdict but since you insist on everyone hearing the full details of your crimes I will schedule a date for the trial with a prosecution and a defence. We will have sentencing upfront as is usual in Wizarding Court.'

Percy's hands were sweating. How could this have happened? Was it Drusilla? Surely even she wouldn't have gone this far, but then she was trying to evict him from his home. What he still didn't know is what had he stolen and from whom?

Judge Ingram looked down at his papers. 'Given

that your debt to your sister and the value of the stolen item match, you had a clear motive for your crime. And there is also the matter of your recent misuse of magic with the elderly. So on balance, a thirty year term in *Noo-gnar* without parole followed with a lifetime ban on any magic use seems fair. We cannot have anyone with magical ability abusing their power and your case will serve as a deterrent to others.'

Percy felt hopeless and small. He'd just wanted to be normal and live a simple life in a quiet part of the world. Now he was condemned to serve most of the rest of his life in the dark and alone. But then, suddenly, Judge Ingram's self-important droning was interrupted by the double doors of the courtroom being dramatically flung open. A small figure, dressed in legal robes and carrying a huge pile of dusty books, stood in the doorway.

Chapter 10

Instant Relief

It was Gladys!

Percy looked up and felt his heart swell. Maybe all was not lost.

She pushed her glasses up her nose and marched fearlessly to the front and addressed the whole courtroom.

'Chief Justice Wizard, Judge Ingram. Judges Primrose and Mudd. People of the Jury, 'I am Percival Balderham's defence counsel and as such I have a legal right to be here for all proceedings. I am therefore somewhat dismayed to see that you have started without me.'

'This is most irregular,' said Judge Primrose.

'I was not informed the guilty party actually had a defence counsel, and commoner one at that. Why weren't they present, Judge Ingram?' queried Judge Mudd.

Percy's old teacher pursed his lips.

'I wasn't sure if they were qualified,' he answered unconvincingly.

Gladys quickly pulled out a folded certificate and handed it across. The three Judges inspected it.

'I was a lawyer for forty years,' Gladys explained, barely containing her disapproving tone of Judge Ingram's underhand tactic. 'I still practise when the need arises. As it has today. I will petition again to use our country's common law given the offence has no magic traces.'

'Out of the question. He is a practitioner of magic,' Judge Primrose replied. 'And there was the matter of him using magic on old people.'

'Yes. Request denied,' said Judge Mudd and handed back Gladys's certificate.

'Agreed,' said Judge Ingram. 'You'll have to brush

up on your *Wizard Law*.' He banged his small wand and looked around the room. 'We'll accelerate proceedings. Tomorrow the prosecution will begin. Dismissed.'

And with that, Judge Ingram got up and left with a swish of his robe, swiftly followed by the other two Judges. The jury and the gallery filed out too leaving Percy with the two J.M.I. officers and his lawyer Gladys.

'No chit-chat now,' one of the officers warned them.

Gladys brought herself up to her full height which barely reached the Officer's chest.

'I'll have you know that I have a legal right to speak to my client. Paragraph 4, section 2, line 7. Would you like me to read it aloud for you?'

Percy stifled his first grin in twenty days as the Officers visibly retreated.

'I had a teacher like that judge,' said one of the officers to Percy, 'a bully I mean. Ain't easy and you don't seem like the usual sort of criminal we drag up here. Now, it ain't my job to judge if you did it or not, but it is my job to uphold the law. Your lawyer can go to your cell, but you haven't got long, alright?'

'Thank you,' Percy whispered after this unexpected kindness and he and Gladys were led down to his cell.

Percy offered Gladys a seat on his thin woven straw mattress. He sat down next to her and he suddenly felt his shoulders sag and a single tear well up in the corner of his eye. He just wanted to go home.

'There, there dear,' said Gladys, 'I can't begin to imagine what you've been through. It's taken longer than I'd hoped to get us access to the files, let alone you.'

'I don't even really know why I'm here,' said Percy putting his head in his hands. 'I've stolen something from someone, apparently. But I don't know what I'm supposed to have stolen. All I know is that I haven't stolen anything. It's my sister, Drusilla, I know it is. Ever since I turned my back on the Wizarding Community, she's been out to get me, but I never imagined she'd go this far. Not *Noo-gnar.*'

Gladys opened a folder full of papers and traced her finger down the first page.

'Do you know a man called Mr Windthrup?' she asked.

Percy looked up. 'Yes, yes I do. A rude man. He was the client at the last plumbing job I did with Bertie.

'Well, it says here that Mr Windthrup has proof that you were in his house at the time his mother's engagement ring went missing. Gold with a large diamond. Very valuable, he says and it was last seen in the kitchen, where you and Bertie were working. He said he'd left it there because he had been cleaning it.'

'I don't remember seeing him clean it, but I did see the ring. I thought at the time it was a strange place to leave it. I didn't take it, I promise. What would I want with a ring? Bertie will vouch for me. Where is he?'

Gladys closed the folder for a moment.

'That's just it, Bertie has gone missing. He hasn't been seen since the day the ring was apparently stolen. The day you did that job for Mr Windthrup. He only returns phone calls with the same message about being on a long and well-earned holiday. There's something fishy going on and I'm going to get to the bottom of it. You've been set up, Percy. Leave it with me,' Gladys went on as she handed Percy one of her delicious home-made iced buns. 'I am going to get you out of here. Trust me.' And with that, she was led out of the cell, leaving Percy all alone with his thoughts (and the bun!).

Chapter 11

Eternity
Or Escape

The dungeon bell tolled. Percy marked off another day, then he heard the same scratching sound from the wall. He got down on all fours.

'Hello!' he whispered.

The scratching stopped for a moment then resumed. Finally, it was followed by a few very loud taps. A bit of mortar skidded across the floor and past Percy's right ear and a small hole appeared. A metal stick-like thing chipped away more mortar, which made the hole bigger.

'This is just another cell I'm afraid. I'd welcome you with a cup of tea but I can't do magic in here,' Percy said to the stranger.

Another chip of stone felt out and a thin hairy leg poked through the hole, quickly followed by three more legs, a body and then four more legs – a spider! It looked up at Percy with its multiple eyes and raised an eyebrow. Percy sat up.

'Hello! I'm Percy. What's your name and what are you doing in my cell?'

'I'm Herbert IV. I got caught up with this guy next door. Well technically he got caught on my web. It's a long story. Now I'm making my escape. I found this safety pin in his shirt pocket and I've been working to get out ever since. No way he is getting out. A commoner in *Noo-gnar*. Figured I'd have better luck in the cell next door.'

Percy raised both his eyebrows in surprise. He wasn't quite sure what to say.

The spider scuttled around the room then jumped up on the thin straw mattress, quickly making himself at home.

'I like what you've done with the place. Plaiting the straw was a nice touch. Does need some cobwebs though. I heard your door open and close earlier. I know some friends on the outside, if you take me on a ride-along next time you go out, I can escape this place. I'll work out something for you in return. What'cha think? You game?' said the Spider with a grin.

'Sure,' Percy said sceptically, 'I haven't got anything to lose!'

As if on cue, the door lock clunked and the hinges screeched and Percy's cell door opened.

'I'll climb into your robe pocket and hide,' whispered Herbert.

Percy's mind suddenly raced. It was all happening so fast. If he could get a message out via Herbert, maybe someone could find Bertie and he could clear his name. Or was it too late? He wasn't sure. Henry, his kindly Gaoler, stood waiting with his lantern.

'Two seconds, Henry. How've you been?' asked Percy as he tried to think.

'Oh you know, so-so. Not much to do these days,' the Gaoler replied as he picked his nose.

Herbert crawled up Percy's leg.

'No wait. Not yet,' Percy hissed, 'I've had an idea. I need you to deliver a message on the outside but I need to tell you what to say. I'll be back, I promise. Wait here and I'll get you out next time.'

The Spider paused, then scurried up to Percy's ear.

'Deal. Don't be long.'

Percy walked into the courtroom. Gladys was there. The gallery was full and the Jury were fidgeting in their seats. As before Judges Mudd and Primrose were already seated.

'All rise,' called the Court Clerk as the Chief Justice Wizard swept grandly into the room.

'Prosecutor. You may begin,' Judge Ingram announced.

A squat goblin with a wicked grin, wearing a blood-red pointy hat pushed his chair back. He pulled out one sheet of paper and paced in front of the Judges as he read from it. Then he turned to the Jury.

'Persons and people of civil society, I bring you a damning tale today. It will leave you feeling unclean, wary of *certain* wizards and disappointed that we failed in our duty to protect everything we hold dear. But fear not, we are here to correct a mistake that has existed since this Wizard was in school. *Noognar* will welcome this liar, this thief, this *manipulator* of magic and minds, with open arms.'

Percy refused to shrink back in shame. He wasn't any of those things, no matter what this Goblin said.

'Objection!' Gladys called out.

'On what grounds?' Judge Ingram snapped.

'He is not a liar,' said Gladys and scribbled something down.

'He has said he is not guilty when he clearly is. That's a lie,' said Judge Primrose.

'That is yet to be proved,' Gladys pointed out.

'He has the right to plead *not guilty*.'

'Argument sustained,' Judge Mudd growled. 'Prosecution. You will not refer to the Defendant as a liar until *after* the final verdict.'

'This yet-to-be proven liar will serve his time for his crime, you'll see,' said the Goblin Prosecutor as he folded his paper and looked at each jury member in turn. 'Percival Balderham was a poor magic student, something that was only revealed when his talented and loyal older sister graduated from school, he no longer had her to cover up his, often dangerous, mistakes. Even with a new wand, he only scraped a pass by the skin of his teeth *but* we don't know how. Foul play, perhaps?'

'He did pass though, didn't he?' Gladys interrupted.

'Barely,' Judge Ingram muttered and looked down.

The Goblin ignored the Judge's intervention and carried on. 'He then decided to forsake all things magical and live with commoners. A most unusual decision to run, like a coward, from his heritage. His loving and afore-mentioned sister, Drusilla, tried to do the right thing. To gently encourage him back to our magical community. But he was having none of it and to his sister's considerable distress, he rudely ignored all her pleas.'

'I wouldn't call buying my home from my landlord and trying to evict me 'gentle,' said Percy indignantly.

The Gallery gasped.

'Silence. I will hold you all in contempt of court if you speak again,' Judge Ingram said and banged his small wand.

The Goblin waited for silence and then continued. 'Instead, this Wizard pretended to be desperate. He got himself into commoner debt by not paying his rent. And then he used his magical abilities to toy with vulnerable old people.' The Goblin shouted the last sentence.

'Objection!' Gladys said.

'Dismissed!' Judge Ingram growled.

'Our magical society does not interfere with commoners. We leave them alone,' said the Goblin, 'but this Wizard did not play by those ancient rules. He slyly convinced a commoner to give him a job.

And why did he want this job? Well, it is not, as his lawyer will tell you, to earn money to pay his rent arrears, oh, no. He wanted this job to create opportunities for himself. Opportunities to steal. And had we not caught him after this first attempt, I quite am sure that he would have continued to pursue a criminal career at the expense of helpless and trusting commoners like poor Mr Windthrup. *Why*, you ask? I wonder as well. But then who can truly understand the motivations of a failed wizard. We are only here to ensure he is punished for his terrible crimes and to keep the public safe from such evil.'

Gladys furiously scribbled another note.

'I call my first witness to the stand. Please tell us your version of events,' said the Goblin.

The floor creaked as Mr Windthrup took his place in the witness box and after a quick glance up at Judge Ingram he began.

'I was having my kitchen refurbished when this Wizard entered my property. He was in the company of my usual plumber, Bertie, his new apprentice, by all accounts. The work was long overdue so I just wanted to get the whole thing over and done with. I offered them tea and biscuits and kindly reminded them that I had to work from home and needed peace and quiet. Well, of course they were rough types so naturally ignored my request and a cacophony of noise followed. It took them twice as long as it should and the workmanship was poor. I should have known. That *Wizard* was rude right from the beginning. I could tell he was looking down on me and everything I've achieved. I've never trusted wizards since . . . um, I mean that Wizard, so when I realised the ring had gone, I just knew it was him!'

'Had you met Percy before that day?' Gladys asked quietly.

'No. No. Thank goodness,' Mr Windthrup replied.

'So when you say *'since'* do you mean your previous experience of the Wizarding Community is unrelated to *this* Wizard?' she copied his intonation then carried on. 'Have you met anyone magical *before* you met Percival Balderham?'

Mr Windthrup tensed his jaw and looked down.

'Objection. Irrelevant line of questioning,' the Goblin piped up.

'Indeed,' concurred Judge Mudd, 'why are you asking?'

'To establish that Mr Windthrup was *against* magical beings *before* meeting Percy and that his prejudice and preconceptions coloured his judgement of my client, Percy Balderham,' Gladys said calmly.

'Please answer the question, Mr Windthrup!' Judge Primrose said before Judge Ingram could bang his wand.

'Yes. I have met others,'

'When?' Gladys asked.

'I applied to go to wizarding school and I was rejected,' Mr Windthrup reluctantly admitted.

'By whom?' asked Gladys as she pushed her glasses up her nose and tapped her pencil on the paper.

'Him!' he whispered as he pointed to Judge Ingram up on his podium.

Everyone in the room gasped!

Percy couldn't believe what he was hearing.

'Order! Order!' shouted Judge Ingram and slammed his wand down three times.

'And what about the stolen ring. Your ring?' the Goblin asked, keen to turn things back to the matter in hand.

Mr Windthrup absently fiddled with something in his jacket pocket then swallowed.

'Of course, yes, well, I was cleaning my late mother's engagement ring in the kitchen when the workman arrived. She left it to me when she passed away. A family heirloom. Worth a lot of money. But more than that, it was a reminder of my dear, dear mother. I left it on the side. It was there when they arrived. I shouldn't have left it there. It was too much temptation for people less successful than myself, but I was busy and had important work to get back to. I forgot about it. I am certain that Wizard took it. Smuggled it out of the kitchen with the rubbish. Of course, I reported him to the authorities immediately. And now I know about his money troubles, it all makes perfect sense.'

The Goblin smiled smugly.

'Thank you. Members of the jury I think you'll agree that this is a clear cut case.'

'Did you see him take it?' Gladys asked.

The Goblin rolled his eyes.

'No,' Mr Windthrup replied.

'So why are you so fixed in your belief that Percy took it and not the other plumber, Bertie? He had just as much opportunity,' said Gladys.

Percy shook his head after that question. Bertie was his friend; he wouldn't steal.

'Well, I just know it,' spluttered Mr Windthrup. 'I'd used Bertie before. He had a reputation to maintain. Whereas this Wizard, he had nothing.'

Gladys crossed out a sentence on her paper and changed tack.

'Without a sink, you had no running water in the kitchen, correct?'

'Correct,' Mr Windthrup replied hesitantly.

'So how were you cleaning the ring in the kitchen? Surely the bathroom would have been better?'

Mr Windthrup's cheeks went red.

'I was trying to, um, I was. Look. It was there.'

'Enough. This man is clearly distressed, you're badgering the witness,' the Goblin interjected.

'Quite,' agreed Judge Ingram. 'No more questions for this witness. Prosecution, please accelerate proceedings. We'll reduce time allowed for additional questions.'

Gladys shot up from her chair.

'Objection!'

Judge Ingram refused to look in her direction.

'Duly noted,' he replied.

Judges Primrose and Mudd looked at each other but remained silent and the Goblin called his next witness.

'Ms Lydia Brown. Mr Balderham's new neighbour. When you first met Percival Balderham, did he seem odd to you?'

Percy's heart leapt at the sight of her, until he remembered about the seal.

'A little,' she replied shyly.

'Did he not *terrify* you when he magicked a real live seal into your bathroom?'

Lydia paused and looked at Percy. A thread of understanding passed between them in that moment. She was sorry and he knew it. For the first time Percy didn't need words. Instead, he smiled.

'Yes, but . . . ' she began.

'Thank you,' the Goblin interrupted, 'no further questions, you may leave.'

Then he strode over to the Jury. Percy looked down. He was condemned and he knew it.

'As you can see,' boomed the Goblin, 'this Wizard used his magic to intimidate an innocent woman in her own home. And my next witness, his postman, will offer further evidence of Mr Balderham's bad character.'

Gladys didn't look up from her notes.

'You deliver this Wizard's mail regularly, correct?' the Goblin asked.

'Yes,' the Postman replied with a look of confusion. 'What's this all about? I was just doing my rounds and some officer made me come here.'

The Goblin narrowed his eyes at the Commoner.

'Did this Wizard thoughtlessly barge into you the other day?'

'Well, um, I suppose so, yes. But . . ."

'Thank you,' the Goblin interrupted, just as he had with Lydia. 'No more questions. Next witness.'

The Goblin looked at the Jury. 'An aggressive streak as well as his dishonesty — the plot thickens.'

Next on the stand was Nurse Jane. She looked like a deer in headlights.

'Percival Balderham visited your institution regularly, did he not?' asked the Goblin.

'Yes.'

'And did he tell you he was a wizard? Did he do tricks? Anything other-worldly?'

'Oh yes! He was very proud of his costume. Though he pretended he wasn't very good, actually I thought it was quite convincing! Turning Reginald into a toad and then both Reg and Frank into beach balls like that. I still don't know how he did it,' smiled the Nurse.

'Objection!' Gladys shouted. 'We asked the defendant to do magic shows. He was volunteering!'

Judge Ingram frowned and some members of the Jury tutted.

'Control yourself, Counsel or I will hold you in contempt of court. I suppose this is to be expected if one allows commoners into our courtroom,' said the Chief Judge.

Gladys sighed. At this rate there was nothing she would be able to do to help her friend. It was so dreadfully unfair. Everything was being twisted to make Percy look guilty.

'At best,' the Goblin went on, with a smile as twisted as the 'facts' he was presenting to the court, 'Percy Balderham was an embarrassment to the Wizarding Community and bringing us *all* into disrepute, at worst, he was cruelly meddling with vulnerable commoners.'

Gladys had a look of thunder on her face but kept her mouth shut as the Goblin strutted cockily across the courtroom.

'I call my last witness,' he announced, 'Percival Balderham.'

Chapter 12

Next Witness

The room fell deathly silent.

Gladys looked up in shock.

Percy was utterly bewildered and made his way
to the witness box in the manner of a condemned
man.

And the Goblin began his cross-examination.

'Did you or did you not, turn some elderly
commoners into beach balls?' he boomed.

'I did,' Percy replied truthfully.

'And did you hit your postman?'

'It was an accident.'

'Answer the question,' the Goblin snapped.

'Yes,' Percy whispered.

The Goblin looked away from Percy to the Jury.

'Did you lie to the Receptionist at the swimming pool and pretend that the problems were caused by a normal leak and not, as was actually the case, a water dragon?'

'Yes, but . . .'

The Goblin cut him off.

'Did you clean up Mr Windthrup's kitchen?'

'Yes,' Percy said in resignation.

'Did you see a ring in Mr Windthrup's kitchen?'

Percy's mind flooded with doubt. Had he seen a ring or hadn't he?

'I'm not sure,' he replied honestly.

'Did you *steal* the ring?' the Prosecutor said with finality.

Percy held his head up and said, 'I did not steal the ring.'

A collective murmur echoed through the chamber.

'I want to cross-examine my client,' said Gladys and stood up.

'Out of the question,' said Judge Ingram cutting her off.

'Then I would like to call additional witnesses for the defence,' Gladys demanded. 'Surely this Wizarding Court wants to dispense justice and to hear both sides of the case?'

The Goblin looked up at the Judges, who in turn looked at each other and then at the bewildered Jury. None of them had ever come across someone like Gladys before.

'We will adjourn for lunch,' Judge Primrose announced, breaking the tension. 'We will decide on our return.'

Chapter 13

Next Door

Henry shut the cell door behind Percy and Gladys. The cold stone and dim light was beginning to feel comfortingly familiar to the Wizard.

'Percy, you're back at last,' said Herbert from his web in the corner.

'Oh! I didn't know you had company down here,' said a rather startled Gladys.

'Herbert IV meet Gladys. Gladys meet Herbert IV,' Percy replied. 'He accidentally got caught with another inmate next door. I'm going to help him escape and in return, I've asked Herbert to deliver a message for me on the outside. Not that it will help much now.'

'Pleasure to meet you,' said the Spider as he scampered down a thread and proffered a hairy leg to Gladys. 'But more importantly, I'm afraid I've got some bad news for you, Percy.'

'How could it get any worse?' Percy asked gloomily.

'Just before you got back from court, there was someone in your cell. Nasty-looking fellow. Grumpy too. A goblin, I think,' said Herbert. 'He searched the clothes you were using for a pillow and shoved something in one of the pockets. I took a look after he'd left, and guess what I found?'

Herbert produced a gold ring with a big diamond. The ring. Mr Windthrup's 'stolen' ring!

'Looks like they were trying to fit you up!' the Spider concluded.

Gladys clapped her hands together. 'That's fantastic!'

'Is it?' asked Percy, confused. 'But they're trying to frame me. We've got to get rid of it! Wait. Herbert could testify! He saw them do it.'

'He could,' Gladys replied. 'But we'd only get the

Goblin and Mr Windthrup at best. And you've seen what the Judges are like. They're totally biased in favour of the Prosecution. They could just as easily dismiss Herbert's testimony. No, we need to be smarter if we want to catch whoever is pulling the strings in the background. I noticed Mr Windthrup fiddling with something in his pocket when he was on the witness stand. I'm certain it was the ring. And I'm also certain he gave it to the Goblin so that he could plant it in here. Nothing else is working and they're getting desperate.' Gladys shuffled her papers and tapped her chin and went on. 'At the moment their argument is twisting the facts to support their version of events. They're trying to scare you into a false confession *or* convince the Jury of your bad character and get a conviction that way. With the ring found in your cell it would have been a done deal but now *we* have it, we have a chance to expose their plot. But what to do next?'

Gladys wracked her brains while Percy paced round the tiny cell with Herbert on his shoulder. The tension was palpable until, finally, the old 'oman spoke again.

'I've managed to get your sister to testify for you,' Gladys began, 'and I've also got Frank and Reginald waiting in the wings if we need them. And we've got the ring. That's the good news, but what we really need is Bertie. He could clear your reputation with the Jury. Instead of being the villain, they'll see you as the victim. Then we turn the tide on Mr Windthrup and hopefully he'll confess everything and we'll find out who he's been working with.'

Percy could hardly believe what he was hearing. Drusilla. Helping him? But why? He was sure she was the architect of all his problems. Not this time, apparently.

'Why is Mr Windthrup out to get me?' Percy asked. 'I don't understand. I never did anything to him. I don't even know him.'

'Because he's a bully, Percy. Bullies do that. They pick on people because it makes them feel powerful when inside they don't feel like that at all. Most bullies are weak cowards inside. It's difficult to face your own fears and doubts. Much easier to sow them in the lives of others. And because you're something that he wanted to be – a wizard. But let's not dwell on that. We have to find Bertie or all is lost. Herbert, any ideas?'

'If you can smuggle me out of here, I can contact my network. What does he look like?' the Spider replied.

Commoner. Really tall. Brown hair. Brown eyes. Rough hands and a big smile. He wears blue overalls like those over there,' Percy said.

Herbert hopped onto Percy's lap then held his forelegs up. 'Tall, you say? Really tall and skinny?'

'Yeah. You'd definitely spot him in a crowd,' said Percy.

'You're not going to believe this,' grinned Herbert, 'but . . .'

'Believe what?' asked Percy.

'Let him finish,' said Gladys and patted Percy's arm.

'Well, the inmate next to you is a really tall commoner and he is wearing blue overalls.'

Percy put Herbert on the stone bed and immediately banged on the thick stone wall. 'Bertie? Bertie! Can you hear me?'

'That won't do any good. It's four feet of solid

stone. Trust me,' said Herbert.

'The hole!' Percy dropped to all fours and shouted into the crack that Herbert had made in the mortar. 'Bertie? Bertie! Can you hear me?'

'Percy? Is that you? Percy! It's awful in here. I've nearly lost my mind,' wailed Bertie.

'It's me! It's good to hear your voice. Give me a sec Bertie,' Percy said and turned to Gladys.

'We need to get him out,' Gladys said. 'The trouble is, this is all obviously part of the plan. They know he is here. If we raise it, they'll deny it or he'll *conveniently* get moved to another place. We need it to appear as if he arrived as a normal witness.'

'Henry the Gaoler will help us,' Percy said confidently. 'But, Herbert, I still need you to contact someone on the outside. It's time to call in a favour.'

Chapter 14

A Moment of Truth?

Back in the courtroom, Percy sat quietly but his limbs were full of energy, like a firework ready to go off. So far their plan had worked. Herbert had successfully scuttled away and Henry had agreed to take Bertie out of his cell for a bit of exercise around the building. Gladys walked purposefully towards Mr Windthrup.

'Oh, I am sorry,' she said as she bumped into him accidentally on purpose. 'By the way I just wanted to ask, Mr Windthrup, the ring you've lost, was the diamond a big one cut into a square shape?'

Mr Windthrup frowned in confusion.

'All rise,' called the Clerk as the three Judges filed in.

'Never mind,' said Gladys and shuffled back to her seat, leaving Mr Windthrup puzzled.

'Let's get on with it, barked Judge Ingram, 'Defence, call your first witness.'

'I call Drusilla Balderham. Percival's sister,' said Gladys.

A young woman took the stand. She looked almost identical to Percy, except for her electric blue spiky hair, which went perfectly with her robe. She winked at Percy. Then Gladys pushed up her glasses and began.

'From your experience of Percy growing up, is he cruel or cunning or conniving?'

Drusilla laughed.

'Quite the opposite. He is a trusting idiot. Easy to tease, slow to anger and frustratingly kind. Are you still using the wand I gave you in school, Percival? Struggling with magic, by chance?' She addressed her brother directly.

Percy opened his mouth to say yes then closed it. Had she tricked him all this time? Surely not!

'No talking to the defendant, Ms Balderham,' said Judge Ingram.

'Sorry, Your Honour, it's just that it was a cheap wand. I bought it as a joke when his wand broke. He was always better at magic than I was. A natural, Mother called him. Could do spells with a swish of his finger unlike most of us! It was my duty as an older sibling to knock him down a peg or two. Anyway, I've had my fun, and come to terms with his talent. So this explains all the *accidental* magic he's done over the years.'

The Jury looked at each other in shock.

'I've got the wand in question right here,' said Judge Ingram and handed it across to Judge Mudd. 'I must say it is a measly excuse for a magical tool but that's hardly a defence.'

'Especially against theft,' the Goblin growled.

'You're missing the point,' said Gladys shuffling in front of the Prosecution. 'It shows that Percival was a victim of sibling rivalry and more and that it shows that his occasional mixed-up magic was the fault of this wand and not my client's malice.'

Judge Mudd held Judge Ingram's hand down before he could dismiss Gladys's point. But before Gladys could go on, the Goblin leapt up and waved a piece of blank paper in the air.

'I have new evidence,' he gasped. 'The Defendant has the ring! He has been hiding it all this time down in his cell. I request an immediate search.'

Percy straightened his back and tried not to panic after the collective outcry from the Gallery.

'Search the cell!' Judge Ingram commanded quickly before anyone could ask why this had happened now and not earlier.

Gladys calmly accepted the ruling with a nod. Percy looked up at the Gallery and wrung his hands. No sign of Henry or Bertie. The quiet seconds became tense minutes. Where were they? Then, just as he was beginning to lose hope, the door at the back of the room creaked open and in walked Henry and Bertie!

'I also have new evidence to present,' Gladys began. 'The testimony of Percival's manager,

Bertalan, who was also at Mr Windthrup's house on the day in question.'

Judge Ingram went as white as a ghost then swallowed.

Bertie and Henry made their way down to the witness stand, closely followed by the Goblin, who was staring intently at Judge Ingram.

'A false alarm from the Prosecution, it would appear. There's no ring in the cell,' said Judge Primrose as she eyed her fellow judges suspiciously.

'Why is the witness in chains?' Judge Mudd asked in his deep, growly voice.

'He was down in the dungeon, Your Honour,' Henry replied.

'A commoner? In *Noo-gnar?* By whose order?' demanded Judge Mudd.

'I'm just a gaoler,' Henry replied and backed away.

Judge Ingram visibly shrank back.

'Bertie, is it?' Judge Primrose said. 'Kindly tell us who put you in our wizarding detention.'

'That man,' said Bertie and pointed to Judge Ingram.

The Jury gasped.

The Gallery oohed and aahed.

Judge Mudd stood up.

'Are you out of your mind, Ingram? This is worse than a wizard stealing a ring! We have NO jurisdiction on commoners and you know it!'

'I had reason to suspect he was an accomplice,' Judge Ingram muttered.

'Did you indeed?' said Judge Primrose, who also stood up. 'I think we should hear this witness's testimony right away.'

Bertie smiled and winked at Percy and told the court everything, right from the moment he first met the bumbling Wizard.

'So the ring was on the kitchen side?' asked Judge Mudd.

'It certainly was. I remember pointing it out to Percy and telling him to be careful. Oh, and I took a photo of it too – just before we left – been there before, accused of stealing. Can't be too careful, you know. It was there when we left. I felt bad for Percy after that job. Mr Windthrup was very rude about wizards and to Percy. I decided I was going to send Percy on a plumbing course but I wanted it to be a surprise. So I dropped him off. I've got the paperwork here,' Bertie pulled it out of his top pocket. 'Next thing I knew, I was at home relaxing when two big guys came in with that man, that judge up there. They blindfolded me and carted me off to your dungeon! I thought it was a prank at first. But then, well, I knew it was serious when it didn't end and nobody let me out. Percival Balderham is not a thief and is not bringing the Wizarding Community into disrepute. He's a good bloke and he makes the best tea I've ever tasted!'

Gladys didn't wait for the Prosecutor to object and held her hand up.

'I call Mr Windthrup.'

'I'm not going anywhere,' he shouted from the back.

Judge Ingram said nothing as Judge Primrose ordered some officers to grab Mr Windthrup.

Gladys took a deep breath and looked at the Jury.

'You framed Percy for a crime, Mr Windthrup, and I have reason to believe that you cut a deal with someone in this very room.'

The room filled with shouts, chatter and banging.

'Order!' shouted Judge Ingram, but it had no effect.

Judge Mudd slammed his meaty fist on the podium with a thud.

The Public Gallery quietened.

Percy bit his lip and Gladys continued.

'I also have reason to believe that you have the ring about your person right now, Mr Windthrup.'

'What on earth makes you think that?' he asked with a hint of smugness.

'I saw you fiddling with it when you gave your testimony earlier. It's in your right pocket. Kindly empty it,' Gladys replied matter-of-factly.

Mr Windthrup put his hand in his pocket. The colour immediately drained from his face. His mouth fell open. His eyes widened in terror as he pulled out the ring!

The whole courtroom erupted.

Judge Ingram shot up.

'Typical!' he boomed, 'a commoner accusing our kind of a terrible crime in order to hide their own guilt! This case is dismissed. Pervical Balderham is innocent.'

Bertie went over to Percy and patted him on the back but Gladys stayed where she was.

'Judges Primrose and Mudd, there is another guilty party in this room. Your colleague, Chief Justice Wizard Ingram.'

The two Judges glanced at each other, unsure what to do. J.M.I. officers appeared at all of the entrances and exits.

'Get them out. All the Commoners out,' ordered a red-faced Judge Ingram.

Then suddenly, a loud thunder clap rocked the court, followed by a flash of lightning. Shouts were replaced with screams and water streamed down windows. Puddles formed near the doors and spread under the chairs. More thunder boomed. The crowd panicked.

All the while Percy sat quietly. *Right on time*, he thought.

A tendril of water opened the main door and Earl, the Water Dragon, glided into the Court.

'A *dragon?*' Judge Ingram gasped.

And with that, Earl rose up to his full height, and glared at the Judges.

'I have been told of a gross miscarriage of justice. Dragons *are* Truth *and* Magic. You may dispense judgement but we are the natural law. How did this happen?'

'You're too late,' snapped Judge Ingram, 'this case is already closed. A commoner issue, nothing important. Certainly nothing Your Lordship should be bothering yourself with. The Defendant is not guilty. See, I've written it here. All a mistake.'

The water rippled and bulged.

'HOW?' the Dragon bellowed.

'It was his idea,' Mr Windthrup screamed and pointed at Judge Ingram.

'Don't you blame me,' said the Judge, 'you started it. You wanted a deal to get you in a wizarding school.'

Percy watched the exchange like a tennis match.

'Oh yeah?' Mr Windthrup snapped. 'You're the one who wanted to punish the Wizard and you're the one who put his friend in the dungeon. You suggested planting the ring. And all because Percy cost you a promotion to headmaster with his accidental magic.'

'That boy was a menace! He turned my head of department into a muddy zebra! I got the blame for his inability to control his magic. For *his* failure.'

'Surely it was your duty to teach him how to use his magic,' said Gladys. 'Percy didn't fail, he was failed. By you! You've broken commoner and magical law.'

Earl looked down at the old lady in surprise. She was quite something.

'Jury of the court, this case is still open,' Judge Primrose called out. 'Judge Ingram and Mr Windthrup are now on trial for their crimes. How do you find them?'

'Guilty,' said a gnome without hesitation.

'Agreed!' added a woman.

Then all of the Jury members said guilty in turn.

'Guilty!' Judge Mudd growled in conclusion. 'Officer, take Ingram down to the dungeon and get me the commoner Police Commissioner.'

'We did it!' laughed Gladys and hugged Percy's middle as the courtroom cleared.

'You did it,' Percy hugged her back.

'I think I played a part,' said Earl with a grin.

'I was the star,' Bertie said.

'Are you kidding?' said Herbert as he spun a web and launched himself off Earl's shoulder. 'It was my daring escape that sealed the deal.'

The old Gaoler cleared his throat.

'Henry!' Percy offered his hand. 'We couldn't have done this without you. Thank you!'

'Begging your pardon,' the Gaoler said as he shook it, 'but I was wondering if our agreement is still valid?'

'It certainly is. Earl,' Percy addressed the Dragon, 'I need you to forgive this man for his crime of stealing dragon's treasure. Only a dragon can do it. He has served his time and regrets his actions.'

'That I do, Your Lordship,' said Henry and bowed his head.

Earl looked down his snout for a moment and narrowed his eyes.

'I feel the truth in you. You are free from Noo-gnar. Besides, we will have a new Gaoler – Ingram!'

Chapter 15

Tea O'Clock

Back outside 124 Rangoon road, Percy opened his familiar gate and raised an eyebrow. All of his furniture was in the front garden, including a table and chairs, and his door was wide open.

'Percy, you're back at last! You took your time!' shouted Magnus as a man emerged carrying him. 'I called Gladys weeks ago. Look, get this guy off, will you? Also did you buy this morning's newspaper? I want to do the crossword. Your mum called. She wasn't happy about Drusilla buying your place.'

Lydia trotted out of the front door and whisked

some books and a clock back inside then waved to Percy.

'You're back! I held the Bailiff off for as long as I could.'

'I'm just doing my job,' the Bailiff complained.

'Don't worry,' said Percy.

Behind him, Bertie, Gladys, Henry, Herbert IV and Drusilla waited.

'What will you do now?' Gladys asked.

'Drusilla? End this now and then we're quits. What do you say? I want my home back. I'll have two new lodgers with Henry and Herbert IV. And I want you to let me live my life as I please,' Percy said.

'Yeah, yeah, alright,' said Drusilla. 'Enough is enough. I'll call the Bailiffs off. And . . .' she tailed off. 'Er, well, um,'

'Spit it out, Drusilla,' said Percy.

'OK. I'm sorry. Alright. Happy now?'

Percy smiled.

'I'd better get going,' Bertie announced, 'I've got some explaining to do myself. I'll pick you up tomorrow, Percy. eight o'clock sharp. We've got some catching up to do with my plumbing jobs.'

'Well, that was thirsty work,' Gladys said, sitting down heavily at Percy's dining room table. 'I think it's Tea O'Clock, isn't it?'

Percy swished his finger and unfolded that morning's newspaper. It *was* time for tea after all. Gladys was right!

Special Thanks

I would like to express my sincerest gratitude to my friends for their quiet and ever-present encouragement of me and my creativity. As always to my wife, Anna. To Bernado, thank you for reading my previous stories – I hope you like Percy's adventure just as much.

Finally to those in the background, quietly chipping off the rough edges with me, thank you Alice & Clair.

About
Atticus Ryder

Atticus Ryder is a writer and illustrator. Born and raised in the countryside, he has been a lifelong fan of practical jokes, Lego, colourful adventures and above all else a good story. Atticus currently lives in the big smoke (London) with his family, taps friends on the opposite shoulder and glues coins to the floor.

Back in secondary school Atticus had the good fortune to bump into Derik the Dragon from Twilight Tales, whose story helped him to win a prize in a short story competition. Over the years other characters like Percy, Bertie and Gladys gave him their stories to tell – now they're here for you.

P.S. He has met some more travellers from magical moments between the sunset and the moonrise. Look out for their stories in Twilight Tales AND *The Minor Gentleman* . . .

Other books by Atticus Ryder

From The Memory Thief to AI Cat One, here are ten adventure-packed stories for children to spark their imaginations and make them laugh. What will happen to Albert the dancing troll as he finds a new home? Or James as he competes in a daring game of intergalactic snakes and ladders? Maybe the Prankster is more than he seems...

Age: 6-99
ISBN: 978-1-83809-562-8

If you heard piano music in the middle of the night,
would you follow the melody into the woods?
See what Lucy does and let her adventure become
yours in this fantastical story where she encounters
Hoot the talking owl, Duchess Thorn and her
musical troupe, mysterious memories bound
in magic and the Minor Gentleman.

Age: 6-99
ISBN: 978-1-83809-560-4

Lightning Source UK Ltd.
Milton Keynes UK
UKHW050008130122
397020UK00014B/595